ISBN 9798507006960



Amy Lynn McConahy

Sunset Valley Books

New Castle, Pennsylvania

www.wbblive.com/sunsetvalleybooks

Facebook: Sunset Valley Books

Instagram: SunsetValleyBooks

For Puzzles & Magnets Visit: www.etsy.com/shop/sunsetvalleybooks

For Other Petey Merchandise Visit: www.redbubble.com/people/sirensmuse/shop

Illustrations by Amy Lynn McConahy

Story by Amy Lynn McConahy

Copyediting by Sarah McConahy

Cover design by Amy Lynn McConahy

Cover Font (Touch of Nature) by Ben McGehee (www.fontspace.com/unauthorized-type)

# REDBUBBLE

**SEARCH:**
**"Petey the Pufferfish"**

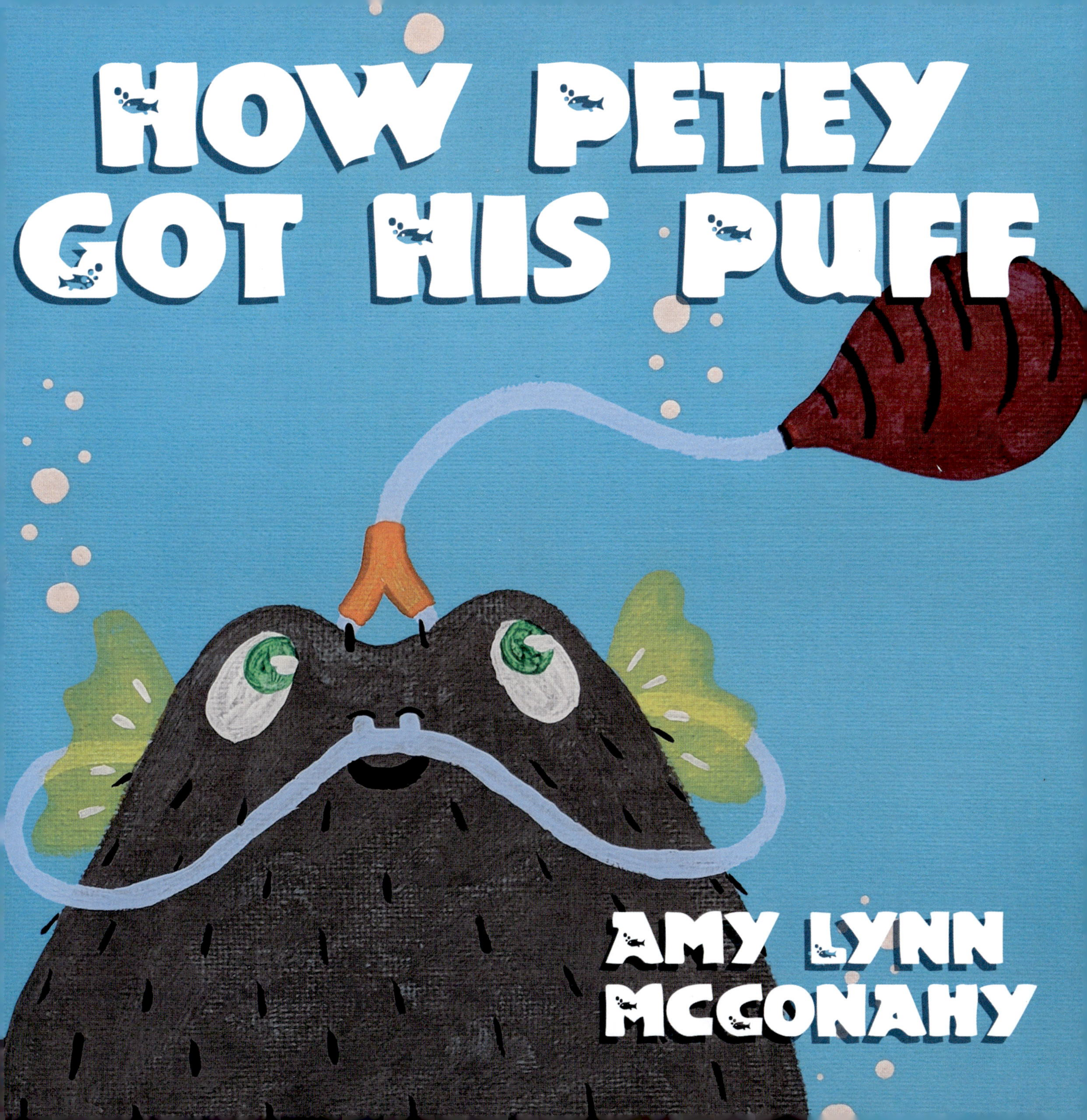
HOW PETEY
GOT HIS PUFF
AMY LYNN
MCCONAHY

Petey the pufferfish was born like any other puffer,
surrounded by many brothers and sisters
in the sandy waters outside of a coral reef.

As Petey and his siblings grew,
they played and frolicked,
munching on clams and algae
to their hearts' content.

As they played, Petey noticed that he was different. You see, as pufferfish grow, they learn to fill their bellies with water to make themselves into a large spiky ball.

Being a large spiky ball
protects a pufferfish
from being eaten
by bigger fish.

As each of Petey's brothers and sisters learned to puff, they would leave to explore the waters of the wide ocean.

One after another they learned to puff,
and soon there was no one left
in their sandy home but Petey.

Petey tried and tried,
but he could not fill his belly on his own.

What Petey did not know was that a friendly oceanographer named Kai had been observing their nest. Kai had watched the puffers grow and leave to explore the waters of the wide ocean. He felt bad for Petey.

Kai saw how hard Petey tried to puff and had an idea how he could help him. The next day Kai brought some special tubes with a ball on the end just for Petey.

Kai gently caught Petey in a net
and placed the special tubes in his nose.
Then Kai showed Petey how to press the ball.

Petey pressed the ball and it filled his belly with water. Slowly, slowly Petey began to puff!

Petey was so excited! Now he could explore the waters of the wide ocean with his brothers and sisters.

With a nod of thanks to Kai,
Petey swam off to find his siblings.

When he found them,
Petey showed how his
wonderful new tubes and ball
allowed to him puff
just like them!

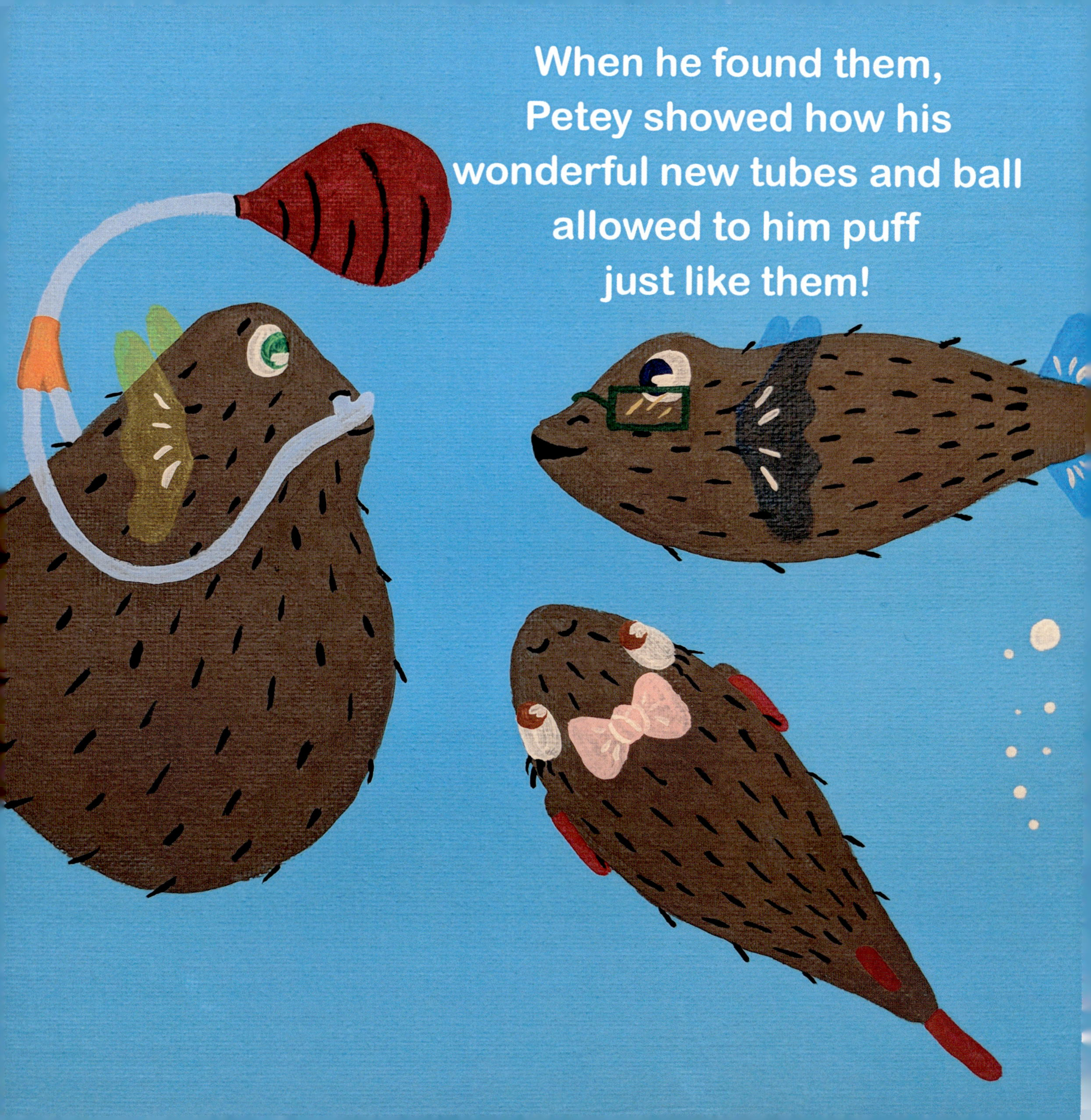

Petey's brothers and sisters looked curiously at his tubes and ball. When they saw how excited Petey was to puff, they were happy too.

"Let's go explore!" Petey said.
And with a flick of their tails,
they swam off to explore the waters
of the wide ocean together.

This book has been written in honor of Nolan, a NEHI warrior, in hopes that it will educate others about oxygen therapy. Hopefully, they will learn to look beyond the nasal cannula and tubes, and see the generous, loving spirit of those who live with rare lung diseases.

Amy Lynn McConahy is a fifth-generation resident of a small town in Pennsylvania. She is a wife, mother of three rambunctious children, a church worship leader, and a majestic maven of the domestic domain. Above all, she is a child of God who is constantly seeking His light. If she would have you take one thing from the reading of "How Petey Got His Puff", it would be hope. Hope that things will get better. Hope found in a God of Love.

# OTHER CHILDREN'S BOOKS BY AMY LYNN

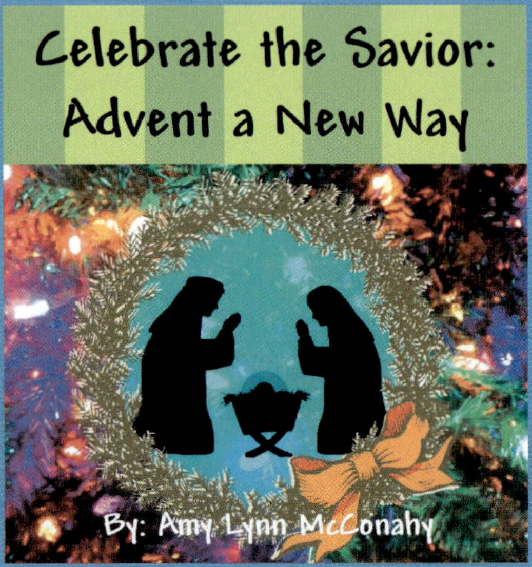

Available on Amazon:
Amy Lynn McConahy
& Etsy:
Sunset Valley Books

Made in the USA
Middletown, DE
17 December 2024

67581088R00015